The Eve
Children

PITKIN COU

D0436500

1 13 0002832458

PITKIN COUNTY LIBRARY

J FICTION T763sL 1 TRUEIT
Trueit, Trudi Strain.   14.99
No girls allowed (dogs okay)

WITHDRAWN

120 NORTH MILL ST. • ASPEN, CO 81611 • (970) 429-1900

SMART TIMES TEN

SCAAAAAAAAAAAAAAB!"

That's my sister, Isabelle. She must have found the hunk of cheddar cheese I stuck in her underwear drawer. It's been there for two and a half days. Remind me to write that down in my inventor's notebook. It's my latest experiment to see how long it takes your sister to find cheese hidden in her underwear drawer.

Isabelle and I are twins. But we are nothing alike. Isabelle is smart times ten. She speaks German. She can say the alphabet backward in less than five seconds. She likes to use big words. It's enough to make you *kotzen*. That's German for "puke."

TRUDI TRUEIT

SeCReTS of a Lab Rat

NO GIRLS ALLOWED
(DOGS OKAY)

ILLUSTRATED BY **JIM PAILLOT**

ALADDIN

NEW YORK   LONDON   TORONTO   SYDNEY

This book is a work of fiction. Any references to historical events, real people, or real locales are used fictitiously. Other names, characters, places, and incidents are the product of the author's imagination, and any resemblance to actual events or locales or persons, living or dead, is entirely coincidental.

ALADDIN

An imprint of Simon & Schuster Children's Publishing Division

1230 Avenue of the Americas, New York, NY 10020

Text copyright © 2009 by Trudi Strain Trueit

Illustrations copyright © 2009 by Jim Paillot

All rights reserved, including the right of reproduction in whole or in part in any form.

ALADDIN and related logo are registered trademarks of Simon & Schuster, Inc.

Designed by Karin Paprocki

The text of this book was set in Minister Light.

Manufactured in the United States of America

First Aladdin edition February 2009

2 4 6 8 10 9 7 5 3

Library of Congress Cataloging-in-Publication Data

Trueit, Trudi Strain.

No girls allowed (dogs okay) / by Trudi Trueit.

p. cm.—(Secrets of a lab rat ; #1)

Summary: Fearless nine-year-old "Scab" McNally tries to get his twin sister's help in convincing their parents to let them get a dog, but when he embarrasses her in school with a particularly obnoxious invention, it looks like he has lost her cooperation forever.

ISBN-13: 978-1-4169-7592-2

ISBN-10: 1-4169-7592-6

[1. Twins—Fiction. 2. Brothers and sisters—Fiction. 3. Behavior—Fiction. 4. Schools—Fiction.]

I. Title. II. Series: Trueit, Trudi. Secrets of a lab rat ; #1.

PZ7.T78124 No 2009

[Fic]—22

2008022329

For Austin,

and every boy who loves a dog.

Or wants to.

★ ACKNOWLEDGMENTS ★

I am so very grateful to Liesa Abrams, an absolute joy of an editor, who saw into Scab's heart. And mine. Thanks to my agent, Rosemary Stimola, for her wise guidance, faith in me, and determination to find the right home for Scab. I am indebted to the delightfully talented Jim Paillot for somehow reading my mind. Thanks also to my family—my parents (a quirky girl's best friends), Jennifer (sister, champion, and a heck of a publicist), Lori Dru (protective big sis) and brother, Dean, for teaching me early on the value of a good adventure, and a fully stocked first aid kit. A special nod goes to the young people who inspire me: Marie, Austin, Trina, Bailey, and Carter—I adore you. And, finally, with love to William, whose smile I live for.

1

This Chapter Has Nothing to Do with My Pants

I'm kicking the leg of the chair outside the vice principal's office. I'm snapping my fingers while kicking the leg of the chair outside the vice principal's office. I'm sounding like a whistling firecracker while snapping my fingers while—

"Scab McNally!"

I stop. Then I start again. This time I kick lightly so Mrs. Lipwart doesn't bark at me. That's not her real name. But who can remember her real name with that pink, knobby thing on her top lip? Whenever Mrs. Lipwart gets mad, the knob changes color. I can make it turn purple.

★ BEWARE! ★

MRS. BRACKEN FIRES SPIT rockets at you through her front teeth. Three-two-one, blastoff!

Mr. Corbett's onion-ring dragon breath will melt off your eyebrows.

Whatever the cafeteria served for lunch yesterday is still stuck in Mr. Bell's beard today.

Ms. Jablinski has only one eyebrow—the left one; see Mr. Corbett.

"Pssst!"

My best friend, Doyle Ferguson, is outside in the hall. I knew he wouldn't forget me. We're both in Miss Sweetandsour's fourth-grade class. That's not her real name either. It's just Miss Sweeten. But she can turn sour in a flash if you flick a gooey snotball at Cloey Zittle. *Ka-zing!*

Doyle edges closer. "How—?"

"Wart!"

He drops. When Mrs. Lipwart goes into the copy room, I wave him in. Doyle crawls toward me. He

looks like a lizard in his green jacket. "How long you in for?" he asks.

"Don't know yet. Are you coming over today if I'm not—?" I pretend to choke myself.

"Can't. We're taking Oscar for his shots."

My throat tightens for real. Oscar is his new wiener dog. I've wanted a dog my whole life. But every time I ask, and I ask a lot, my parents say the same thing.

"Someday, Squiggle Bear," says my mom, "when you're older."

"Someday," says my dad, "when you show you can be responsible for a pet."

I'll be ten in two months and nine days. That's double digits! How much more responsible can I get?

By the way, you did *not* hear my mom call me Squiggle Bear.

"You could come with us to the vet," offers Doyle.

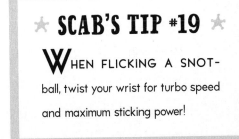

★ **SCAB'S TIP #19** ★

WHEN FLICKING A SNOT-ball, twist your wrist for turbo speed and maximum sticking power!

★ 3 ★

I nod toward the vice principal's door. "What if I'm—?"

"You won't. You'll get out of it."

He's right. I'll wriggle my way out of trouble. I always do. Doyle knows me from the bones out. And I know him from the bones out too. We met at summer day camp when we were seven. I got 148 mosquito bites in four days at camp. We counted them. The best part is that 148 red, oozing, swollen bites equals 148 scabs—scabs that you *have* to scratch and pick at until you peel off every last brown crusty covering. Oh, yeah! After that, Doyle started calling me Scab, and the nickname stuck. That's another reason why he's my best friend. If it weren't for him, people would be calling me by my real name! Sorry, my real name is top secret. You'll have to get special clearance if you want to know it.

"Doyle Ferguson!"

Bug spit! The lip knob has caught us. "Get back to the lunchroom this instant," snaps Mrs. Lipwart, "unless you'd like to join Mr. McNally here."

Doyle spins on his stomach and squirms out

of the office. Mrs. Lipwart starts stapling papers. *Ka-chunk. Ka-chunk.* I go back to softly kicking the leg of the chair outside the vice principal's office. Mr. Huckabee likes to make you wait. He thinks the longer you wait, the more scared you'll be when

TOP SECRET: ★ SCAB'S REAL NAME! ★

ARE YOU A TEACHER? ACCESS DENIED.

Are you a doctor? Access denied.

Are you an adult? Access denied.

Are you a kid with a name you hate too? Access allowed.

My real name is Salvatore Wallingford McNally. Kids were calling me Sally McNally from the second I stepped onto the playground. What were my parents thinking? Spit-swear you'll never tell anyone my name and destroy this top-secret info immediately! If you could eat it, I'd really appreciate it. Put some chocolate syrup or peanut butter on the page or something. Thanks.

★ MY MOST DANGEROUS STUNTS ★

★ Going down Kamikaze Hill at eighty miles per hour my first time on a snowboard. Where are the brakes?

★ Letting a tarantula crawl over my face at the zoo. It made my sister pass out!

★ Hanging upside down on a broken roller coaster for five and a half hours. All the blood rushes to your head. Cool!

★ Flying ten feet, nine inches off Alec Ichikawa's Super Colossal Dirt Bike Ramp. A new world record!

★ Not crying once while getting five stitches in my knee after I flew off Alec's Super Colossal Dirt Bike Ramp.

he calls you in. Not me. I don't scare easily.

"Ka-chunk," I sing with the stapler. "Ka-chunk, ka-chunk. Your feet smell like a skunk."

Mr. Huckabee's bald head appears. It's extra shiny today. I'll bet he uses car wax on it. He tells me to come inside.

"Scab, what is proper behavior during an assembly?"

"Don't smack anybody, even if Lewis Pigford smacks you first."

"Yes, but—"

"Don't jump around like a frog, even if you gotta pee."

"No. Well, yes, that's true, but—"

"I got in trouble for that last time, though I didn't have to pee."

"I think you're missing—"

"See, my teacher *thought* I had to pee and she got mad that I didn't go before we got to the assembly because we'd all made a special bathroom stop. But I had on these new pants my mom made me wear for the school picture and—"

"Scab—"

"I guess they had wool in them or something because I got these little red bumps all over my legs and I was itching like crazy—"

"SCAB!"

"What?"

"I am not interested in your pants."

I slump down. Well, he started it.

"I was talking about your . . . uh . . . performance at the assembly."

Why didn't he say so in the first place? Right now, I ought to be having a contest with Will Greenleaf to see who can toss the most Tater Tots into Cloey Zittle's hood. Will is my second best friend, after Doyle. The three of us go fishing together every Saturday.

Teachers have their own secret code. It's not easy to crack, but I am getting pretty good at it.

"I hear you were making noise while the orchestra was playing."

"No," I say. It wasn't "noise." It was music. My music. I can arm-fart the national anthem.

"Your teacher says you were disruptive."

My armpit was in tune, which is more than

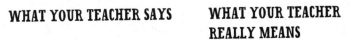

★ CRACKING THE TEACHER CODE ★

WHAT YOUR TEACHER SAYS	WHAT YOUR TEACHER REALLY MEANS
Your drawing is interesting.	It looks like a furball my cat barfed up.
Be courteous to your neighbor.	Poke one more person with that ruler and your butt is fried.
Do your best work.	What you turned in last week was pretty stinky.
Please take this note home to your parents.	You're in big trouble now.
People, let's use our inside voices.	SHUT UP!

I can say for my sister and the rest of the violins. *Squeeeeeeeeak!* Try "The Star-Mangled Banner."

"Scab, if you can't be considerate, you'll have to go to the time-out room during school assemblies. Do you want that?"

"No."

"I want nothing less than your best behavior at the next assembly . . ."

Out of the corner of my eye, I see something outside the window. "Uh-huh."

". . . and I expect you to be cooperative, quiet, and respectful . . ."

It's a dog! In the park across the street, a collie is chasing a tennis ball. He grabs it, turns, and runs to a lady in white pants. She throws the ball again. The dog zips between two maple trees to get it. As he runs, his rusty brown–and-white fur waves in the wind. I bet his fur is soft. I bet it is *so* soft. I'd give anything to be on the other side of this window. Mr. Huckabee is still jabbering. ". . . part of growing up is being aware of your actions and how they affect others. You can't always do what you want to do when you want to do it. Do you see that, Scab?"

"Uh-huh."

Outside, the lady drops to her knees. She wraps her arms around the collie's neck. He licks her cheek with a big, pink, wet tongue. She laughs. She looks so happy.

My heart hurts.

That's what I want. I want a dog to love.

I want a dog to love me back.

CHAPTER

2

Scab's Lab, Part I

SCAAAAAAAAAAAAAAB!"

That's my sister, Isabelle. She must have found the hunk of cheddar cheese I stuck in her underwear drawer. It's been there for two and a half days. Remind me to write that down in my inventor's notebook. It's my latest experiment to see how long it takes your sister to find cheese hidden in her underwear drawer.

Isabelle and I are twins. But we are nothing alike. Isabelle is smart times ten. She speaks German. She can say the alphabet backward in less than five seconds. She likes to use big words. It's enough to make you *kotzen*. That's German for "puke."

My sister got moved up a grade this year. She's in the fifth grade instead of the fourth with me. Miss Sweetandsour says I would do better in school too if I "applied myself." I don't know exactly what that means, but it sounds about as fun as a flu shot. My lab is a mess, but I like it that way. Isabelle freaks out if there's even a pine needle on her floor. My sister is a nervous person. Doyle says she is "wound pretty tight." Getting someone like Isabelle to unwind could take *a lot* of cheese.

"Scaaaaaaaab!"

She's close. I grab the spray bottle off my desk, hold it up, and squeeze the trigger. I sneak into my cave and slide the door shut.

"I know you're in here—gross, what is this goop on the floor?"

A blackberry Fruit Roll-Up. It's my wormhole to outer space. Next question?

"Scab, I know you're in here. When Mom gets home, I'm telling her about the— Ewww!"

She's caught a whiff of my new stinky sister-be-gone spray. I made it to keep Isabelle out of my lab when I'm not around. I've been working on the spray for a whole month. It's not perfect. After all, it's been ten seconds and she's *still* here. I'm shooting for five seconds tops.

Bug spit! I smell fresh air. Isabelle has opened a window.

ISABELLE'S SMELL
★ SISTER-BE-GONE SPRAY ★

1 cup used bathwater

1 cup cabbage stew or any slimy soup

½ cup vinegar

1 packet of taco sauce mix

3 slices of bologna (meat loaf works too)

8 dandelions

2 spoonfuls of mayonnaise

4 Junior Mints

Mix everything in a blender until there are no more chunks.

Pour into empty spray bottle. Spray once in direction of sister.

Watch sister scram!

I'd better go out there before she starts snooping through my stuff.

My sister is holding her nose. "It's noisome in here."

"Huh?"

"Stinky."

"I don't smell anything weird."

"You wouldn't. I'm telling Mom and Dad about the mustard you put in my cheetah purse."

I laugh. That wasn't an experiment. That was a dare from Doyle.

"I'm also telling about your arm-farting at the assembly." She lets go of her nose. "It's all in my report. It's printing out now."

Double bug spit! My sister takes notes on everything I do. She writes up a news report and turns it in to my parents. Sometimes Isabelle reads it out loud like she is Katie Couric or something.

I aim my Nerf gun at her and fire. I get off three shots. Two of the yellow balls bounce off her shoulder. The other hits her in the nose. Sweet!

"I'm putting that in my report."

"I don't care." I say it like I mean it, and most of the time I do. But sometimes I wish my sister would say something nice about me in her report. She never will.

"Hey, Izzy—"

"I told you not to call me that anymore."

★ SCAB NEWS ★

BY ISABELLE C. MCNALLY (A+ STUDENT)

★ 8:05 a.m.: Scab crossed Larkspur Avenue before the light changed. I told him not to.

★ 10:13 a.m.: At first recess, Scab went to the big pretzel oak tree with Doyle and Will, which is against school rules. I told him not to.

★ 11:24 a.m.: Scab stood up during the spring assembly and arm-farted "The Star-Spangled Banner" along with my orchestra. He danced around like a chicken. It was awful!! Miss Sweeten made him go to the vice principal's office.

★ 12:19 p.m.: Scab got off without detention. I knew he would. It is this reporter's opinion that Scab gets away with EVERYTHING.

★ 3:47 p.m.: Scab ruined my favorite cheetah purse!

THIS CONCLUDES SCAB NEWS FOR TODAY. ISABELLE CATHERINE McNally reporting.

P.S. 3:59 p.m.: Scab shot me in the nose with his Nerf gun.

P.P.S. Scab's room really smells. I think a rat died in there.

"Is-a-belle, did you hear? Mom and Dad took out an ad in the *Granite Falls Gazette*."

Her eyes grow. "They did?"

"We're trading you for a dog."

"Very funny. I want a cat like Laura's. Princess Bonbon Fancypaws is a white Persian. She is sooooo adorable. She wears a pink collar with a cute little bow. . . ."

I flip my Seahawks helmet, lean over it, and pretend to retch my guts out.

"You are such a *Pilobolus*, Scab. You probably don't even know what that means, which makes you a dumb *Pilobolus*."

"I know what a pile of buses is."

"Puh-LAH-bull-uss." She sounds it out for me like I'm two. "It's a type of fungus. I just called you a fungus."

Actually, she called me a dumb fungus.

I grin. "We're twins, so if I'm a fungus, what are you?"

Isabelle ignores me. *"Auf Wiedersehen, Erdnusskopf."* That sentence I know. It means "see ya, peanuthead" in German. I get that one a lot.

"Izzy, wait." I don't want her to leave mad. "I'll buy you a new cheetah purse. How much is it?"

"Twenty-five dollars."

"Twenty-five bucks? For a crummy purse?"

"I knew you wouldn't pay for it."

"All I've got is nine dollars and twelve cents. Take it or leave it."

> ★ **FOR SALE** ★
>
> ONE TWIN SISTER. nine years, ten months old. Brown hair. Blue eyes. Smart. Good memory. Missing sense of humor. House-trained. Will trade for dog that is same. Any breed. Phone 555-7078. Ask for Scab. Hurry.

She kicks at a leg that's broken off my big *Tyrannosaurus rex* model. "Take it."

"Want to shoot some hoops? Let's play Horse."

Isabelle doesn't say anything. But she doesn't go, either.

"I'll even take an *H* to start," I say.

"Don't do me any favors. I'll beat you fair and square."

I fish my basketball out of the bottom of pile number two. I toss it to Isabelle. She catches it. "I'm still giving Mom and Dad my report." She tucks the ball under her arm as she leaves. "And you're still a *Pilobolus*."

My sister thinks *I'm* fungus?

Wait till she finds the cheese in her underwear drawer.

3

Baaaad Dog, Gooood Idea

Oscar is asleep in my lap. His short, coppery red fur shines in the sun. I stroke one of his floppy ears and his nose twitches. Doyle is so lucky. I've watched how Oscar races out of the house when Doyle gets home from school. His tail wags a zillion times a minute. He becomes a tornado of joy—spinning, spinning, spinning! That's why I want a dog. A dog loves you even if you aren't smart times ten or don't know how to say the alphabet backward. A dog loves you because you are you.

"Banana peel." Doyle is calling from inside my family's trash can.

★ **HOT DOG FACTS** ★

O SCAR IS A DACHSHUND (DOCKS-HUNT). IT'S A German word that means "badger dog." Dachshunds were once used to help people hunt for badgers and other small animals (but not anymore). Miniature dachshunds weigh twelve pounds or less. I bet my sister's head weighs more than Oscar. Make way for the world's biggest brain!

"No," I say.

"Tea bag?"

"Nope."

"Hey, look! Soggy potato skins."

"Not stinky enough." I need a megasmelly secret ingredient to finish Isabelle's Smell.

"Wait . . . I think I've got something. . . . Oh, geez." Doyle stands up. White goop is dripping from his fingers. "This had better be clam chowder, Scab."

"I guess we should try Mr. Dawber's can."

"You try it. I've had enough fun going through

your garbage." He wipes his hands on his jeans. "I've got to walk Oscar."

I gently nudge Oscar until his eyes open. "Hey, buddy," I whisper. But his sleepy eyes aren't looking at me. They are locked on to Doyle. "I'll walk him," I say, trying not to sound jealous.

"Are you sure?"

Am I sure? Am I *sure*?

"I'd better come with you."

How hard can it be to walk a dog? But Oscar is Doyle's dog, so I keep quiet. Doyle snaps Oscar's leash on him and hands it to me. Sweet!

One thing I learn pretty quickly. You don't walk a dog. A dog walks you. Oscar's squatty legs zigzag down the sidewalk. He stops to sniff everything. And I mean *everything*.

"How long does it take to walk him?" I ask.

"About a half hour—"

"That's not so bad."

"Three times a day."

"Three times?"

PITKIN COUNTY LIBRARY
120 NORTH MILL STREET
ASPEN, COLORADO 81611

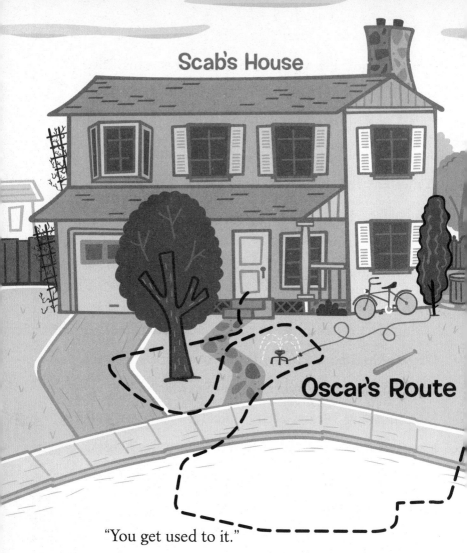

Scab's House

Oscar's Route

"You get used to it."

"R-rruff," says Oscar. I don't think he likes us talking about him.

"We could walk our dogs together, if you had a dog," says Doyle.

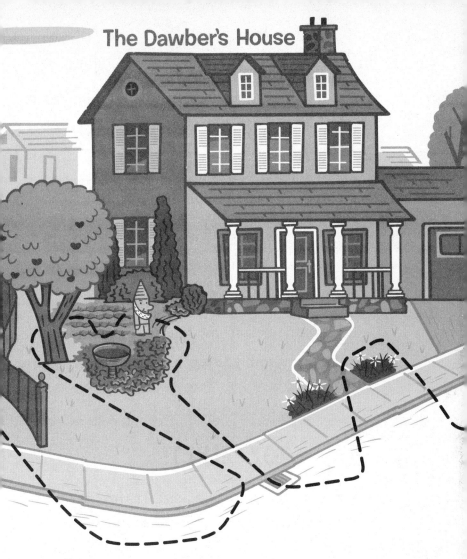

The Dawber's House

"I'll get one."

"You always say that."

"This time, I've got a plan. See, I'm going to save up to buy a dog. Once my mom and dad see how responsible I am with money, they'll know I'm responsible enough to take care of a pet. They'll *have* to say yes."

Doyle agrees.

"How much did Oscar cost?" I ask.

"We got him at the shelter in Arlington. I think he was about sixty bucks."

"Bug spit."

"How much have you got?"

"I *had* nine dollars and twelve cents in my safe. I had to give it to my sister." I see his frown. "Don't ask."

★ TOP SECRET! ★

SAFE IS LOCATED IN MY LIFE-SIZE FRANKENSTEIN monster head with "amazingly realistic" removable gel brain. Brain was lost last summer.*

Safe location: Under loose floorboards 2 feet, 7 ¾ inches from southwest corner of window.

*check pile number four.

"You know what?" Doyle's face brightens. "You ought to get Isabelle to ask for your dog."

"My sister? Why?"

"You've already tried, like what, eight times this year?"

"Seven," I lie. It's really nine. "I don't need Isabelle. I can get my own dog."

Oscar is barking.

"All I'm saying is that your sister could be a big help," says Doyle. "She's got the smarts. She'll know what to say. Plus, she's really responsible, and you . . ."

I wait for him to finish so I can kick him in the calf.

"Arf, arf." Oscar is tugging on his leash.

"Wuh-oh," says Doyle.

A black Doberman is galloping down the sidewalk toward us. Lewis Pigford is stumbling after the dog, trying to hold on to its red leash. "Stop, Dimples! Stop!" Lewis trips. He nearly falls sideways into a big rosebush.

I slap my thigh and laugh. It serves Lewis right. The guy is always picking on some poor kid. And usually that kid is shier, shorter, or younger than Lewis.

Doyle, however, isn't laughing. "Dimples is bad news. Let's get out of here." He starts walking away.

I gently pull on Oscar's leash to turn him around. But he has seen Dimples too.

"Oscar, let's go," I say.

He doesn't budge. He just barks faster. And louder. "Arf, arf, arf!" I can't tell if he wants to play with Dimples or fight him. Neither idea is good.

"Oscar, that's a bad idea. That dog will eat you for lunch," I say, yanking on the leash.

Oscar is too busy barking to listen to reason.

"Scab," Doyle shouts over his shoulder, "come *on!*"

Dimples is half a block away. He's charging at full speed. Doyle is right. We need to get out of here. But what do you do when you are locked in a tug-of-war with a stubborn wiener dog? "Doyle!" I cry. "Help!"

My best friend is beside me. He scoops Oscar up in his arms. He unhooks the leash. "Run, Scab! RUN!"

He doesn't have to tell me twice. I pick up my feet

and stay on Doyle's heels. Suddenly I am skidding chin first across the sidewalk. Concrete is ripping into my chin and palms. "Owwwww!"

I skid to a stop and roll over. Oscar's leash is wrapped around my knees. It's tangled in a knot. The more I grab, the tighter the knot gets. Dimples is barreling down on me. His red leash is flying free. Where is Lewis? What happened to Lewis? My fingers can't seem to do anything right. I can't get loose!

Woof! Woof! WOOF! The bark thunders in my head. I see black eyes and sharp teeth and globs of drool. And they're all coming straight for my throat.

"Get up! *Get up!*" yells Doyle.

Kicking wildly, I break free of the leash. I bolt for the maple tree in Mrs. Carbanito's front yard and pull myself up into the V of the trunk. I am clawing bark when I feel Dimples's jaw clamp on to the leg of my jeans. He pulls. I kick. I kick *hard*. I hear the rip of denim. Branches are scratching my face, neck, and arms. I keep jerking my leg with everything I've got, trying to shake the dog loose. On my fourth kick

★ **30** ★

I feel air. That's it! Dimples has let go! I climb like my life depends on it, which it pretty much does. I don't look down until I am a good fifteen feet off the ground.

Woof! Dimples is jumping up on the trunk. *Woof! Woof!*

Each bark sends a bolt of fear through me. Standing on a thick branch, I hug the trunk. My arms are scraped up. My knees are shaking. My mouth feels weird. Sort of wet. Blood?

Dimples circles the tree. He looks up at me hungrily. He growls. After a few tense minutes of glaring and growling, he trots away. Just like that, he trots away. Like I am a toy he's tired of playing with.

I close my eyes. I don't move. Not for a long, long time.

"Scab?" Doyle's voice floats up to me. "You okay?"

"I'm all right." I don't sound like me. I sound like Isabelle.

"You coming down?"

I take my time getting out of the tree 'cause my hands are sore and my legs are still noodles. There's a big hole in the back right leg of my jeans.

"You cut your chin up good," says Doyle. He's holding out a couple of plastic grocery bags to catch the blood.

"I'm okay," I say. I wipe my face on the bottom of my T-shirt.

Doyle is still trying to hand me the bags.

"Really, I'm fine."

He shakes them. "They aren't for you."

I don't get it.

"You wanted to walk him." My best friend nods toward his dog. Oscar is pooping in the middle of Mrs. Carbanito's orange pansies. He's parking a couple of steamy ones beside a spinning plastic rooster.

I stare at Doyle. He doesn't expect *me* to—

"Pick it up," he says. "It's the law."

He does!

Oscar is done. I, however, am still staring at Doyle.

Doyle sighs. "Do you want a dog or don't you?"

I am beginning to wonder. Even so, I snatch the bags from him.

"Use the first bag like a glove to grab the poop and put it in the second bag," instructs my best friend. "Then put the first bag inside the second bag and tie it up tight."

I reach out. I grab. It's a little squishy. And a lot noisome, as Isabelle would say. Even the plastic rooster is looking the other way.

"What do you feed this dog?" I fling the poop into the bag. "This is the most disgusting stuff I've ever—"

I look up at Doyle. We're both thinking the same thing. This is it. We've done it! At last, we've found the final ingredient for Isabelle's Smell.

CHAPTER

4

Super Spy Strikes Again

"Did you bring it?"

"Yep."

Doyle wiggles his fingers. "Hand it over. I mean, smell it over!"

I look around the playground for Isabelle's fluffy pink coat. I don't see it. Of course, that doesn't mean she isn't lurking somewhere. My sister is a good lurker. I unzip my jacket pocket.

Doyle looks confused. "Where is it?"

"I couldn't bring the big sprayer. I ride the bus with Super Spy, remember?"

"Right."

The plastic spray bottle I take out of my pocket is

about five inches tall. My dad has a bunch of these scattered all over the house. They hold the liquid cleaner for his eyeglasses. I snagged one that was almost empty to fill with my new formula for Isabelle's Smell.

I hold up the bottle. "Ready?"

Doyle leans forward.

I take off the black cap. "Set."

He sticks his nose in the air.

"Go!" I pump once.

A thick, grayish brown cloud floats between us.

"Pee-eeew!" Doyle shrieks. He stumbles backward.

Coughing, I put the cap back on the bottle. My eyes are stinging, but I can see that a group of second graders have noticed us. I grab my best friend, spin him around, and we start walking across the playground.

★ ISABELLE: SUPER SPY! ★

★ **X-RAY EYES** see through backpacks, lunch bags, and classroom walls

★ **DOLPHIN SUPERSENSITIVE EARS** hear me burp from a mile away

★ **GIGANTOR BRAIN** remembers every toy of hers I've broken since we were two

★ **FLYING FINGERS** take notes faster than a speeding spit wad

★ **MEGAMOUTH** tattles before I've even finished making the spit wad

★ **FEET OF FIRE** race from the playground to the vice principal's office in 3.7 seconds! Whooooosh!

★ MY INVENTIONS ★

INVENTION	GOOD THING	BAD THING
licorice toothpaste	tastes great	black teeth
peanut butter root beer	my two favorite foods	lumpy root beer
squirrel parachute	saves baby squirrels from falling out of nests	Mom won't let me test it out on squirrels
bite-proof shark suit	if you look like a shark in the water, real sharks won't attack, right?	Mom won't let me test it out on my sister
sister-be-gone spray (Isabelle's Smell)	stinks like crazy	doesn't last long enough; sister comes back

"That stuff is rank," says Doyle, filling his lungs with fresh air. "You did it, Scab. You finally invented something good. Sorry, I didn't mean—"

"I know." He's right. Not all of my inventions are brilliant. Okay, most of them are disasters. But you can't give up. I learned that after I read about an American engineer named Richard James. He was working with springs, trying to design a meter for battleships. Mr. James accidentally dropped one of the springs on the floor and saw that it kept moving on its own. Tada! The Slinky was born. Who knows? Maybe someday one of my accidents will turn out to be something important.

I see pink! It's Isabelle, all right. She is sitting on the bottom step of the orchestra portable. Her head is bent over her notebook. Bug spit! I am too late. She is already writing her news report. Super Spy has struck again.

I shove the spray bottle at Doyle. "Take this. I'll be right back."

"Okay."

"Keep it out of sight. And don't talk to anybody. Not even Will." He'll want to know all the details. I'm not ready to share my invention quite yet, even with my second best friend.

"Okay."

"I mean it, Doyle." My best friend has a problem keeping secrets.

"I said okay."

I sneak up on my sister. "Hi, Izzy."

She slaps the notebook to her chest. "I told you—"

"Is-a-belle, what are you writing?"

"Nothing." She looks guilty.

"If it's another report about me—"

"It's not." She narrows her eyes. "Why? What did you do?"

Now it's my turn to say, "Nothing," and look guilty. It's strange to see Isabelle alone. At recess my sister is usually glued to her two best friends, Kendall Peters and Laura Ling. The girls are still fourth graders, but all the upper grades have the same recess. "So if you're not writing Scab News, why are you over here by yourself?"

"Okay, okay." Isabelle makes a big X on the page with a red felt-tip pen. "I guess I can forget it *this* time. But . . . uh . . . stop . . . throwing away your orange at lunch." She shuts her notebook.

Now I *am* confused. Isabelle *never* forgets anything, especially when it comes to my behavior. But I don't have time to ask her what's going on. Doyle, Will, Lewis, Alec, and Henry are coming this way. My stomach knots up. I need to get rid of my spying sister. Fast!

"Don't you have anyone to play with?" I ask

★ HOW SISTERS MAKE ★ YOU CRAZY!

* They never want to do anything fun, like catch grasshoppers or make a mud fort.

* They hog the bathroom for two hours and come out looking EXACTLY the same as when they went in.

* They want to play beauty shop and curl your hair. NO WAY!

* They expect you to remember where you hid the heads to their dolls. (Check my mud fort.)

Isabelle, still wondering why Laura and Kendall haven't shown up. Even girls don't take this long to go to the bathroom.

"Oh, sure. Sure I do." She checks her watch. "Uh . . . I almost forgot. I told Jenna Lucas and Libby Miles I'd play foursquare. I . . . uh . . . I'd better get going."

"Bye." I shoo her along as the guys close in.

Alec slaps me on the back. "That's a mighty pukey spray you got there, Scab."

"Thanks." I glare at Doyle. Two seconds. I leave the guy alone for two seconds.

"My little brother is always stealing my model airplane paint," Alec says. "This will teach him to keep his slimy mitts off my stuff."

"Mine gets into my baseball cards," says Will.

"I have to share a room with my baby sister," pipes Henry Mapanoo. "She's three."

Everybody groans.

"So what's in it?" asks Will.

I shrink back. I knew it. He wants the scoop, of

★ SCAB'S TIP #4 ★

IF YOUR SISTER WANTS EVERY-
thing you have, the next time you get a
bag of Gummi frogs, bite the head off
each one. She won't dare touch them.
Let's hear it for boy germs!

course. He's always interested in my inventions, which is one reason why I like him. But now is not the time. "Just some stuff," I say. "A little of this and a little of that." I signal him that I will share more later. I don't want to say too much in front of the other guys.

Lewis Pigford punches me. "So what do you want for it, Scab?"

"Want?"

He starts digging in the pocket of his jeans. "Yeah, how much?"

I didn't plan on selling my sister repellant, especially to a gooberhead like Lewis.

Doyle elbows me. I can tell by the way his eyebrows are going up and down that he thinks I should do it. I scan the playground for a fluffy pink coat. I don't see it. What I *do* see is Lewis holding out several crumpled dollar bills. At first I think it's play money, but it's real, all right. Everyone's looking at me.

I bite my lip. "Three bucks?"

Lewis hands me three one-dollar bills. Bug spit! I should have said five.

Doyle gives him the bottle.

"Spray once," I warn Lewis. "It's strong stuff."

"Got it."

"Don't spray it at school. If a teacher catches you with it—"

"Relax, McNally. I can handle teachers."

"What about the rest of us?" asks Will.

I have to spit-swear with Will, Alec, and Henry that I'll bring a bottle for each of them tomorrow. By the time I am done swearing, I have no saliva left.

"Four orders." Doyle whistles. "That's twelve bucks."

It's more than twelve bucks. It's one fifth of a new dog. Sweet!

"You guys coming to play kickball?" calls Will.

Doyle and I race to the soccer field. I'm going to kick that ball to the moon, that's how great I feel. We run past Jenna, Libby, and their friends playing foursquare. I don't see a fluffy pink coat anywhere, which is weird. You know what's weirder? I didn't have an orange in my lunch today. Or yesterday. Or the day before that. It's not like Isabelle to make such a big mistake. My sister never makes mistakes. Trust me.

CHAPTER
5

Whizzing Bats or
a Lemon Tea Party?

S cab?" My mom is knocking on my lab door.
"Do you have my blender in there?"

I look at the plastic pitcher filled with brownish gray goo. "Uh . . . I might."

"I want it back."

She might change her mind if she knew *what* was in her blender. "Okay," I say.

"Dinner's ready."

"In a sec." I am gluing labels onto bottles of Isabelle's Smell. It's been a busy week. After we

★ **ISABELLE'S SMELL** ★
A SISTER-BE-GONE SPRAY
BY SCAB MCNALLY

Directions: SPRAY ONCE TO GET RID OF annoying sister (or little brother).

Warning: Do not spray toward eyes, do not spill on skin, and definitely do not drink!

sold the first batch to Will and the guys, Doyle rounded up a bunch of new orders for my sister-repellant spray. It won't be long before I have enough money to buy my dog. At last! I have been thinking. I suppose it couldn't hurt to have Isabelle help me ask our parents for a dog. But how do I get her to do it? If I want chocolate cake, she wants apple pie. If I want to play mini golf, she wants to roller-skate. If I want a dog, she wants a cat. I wish I had a little brother to look up to me instead of a twin sister, who's always looking down on me.

"Scab!" Isabelle is shouting. "Uncle Ant is here."

I rocket out of my chair.

When it comes to inventing, I take after my uncle Ant. He's a bug exterminator, which is how he got the nickname. Uncle Ant invented a formula to get rid of moles (you know, those tunneling animals that make dirt mounds all over the grass). His special pellets give moles a tummy ache so they go to someone else's yard.

"Scab-o!" My uncle wrestles me to the floor. He sees the cut on my chin. "What's this? Looks like you're living up to your name, kiddo."

"Scab tangled with the Pigfords' Doberman," says my dad. He is going through the top drawer of the computer desk.

"I wasn't afraid," I say, flexing my biceps.

My sister chuckles. "That's not what I heard, Monkey Boy."

"Eat termites, Isabelle."

"You first."

"Actually," says Uncle Ant, "termites are tasty. Pound for pound they have more protein than a hamburger. They are fun to eat, too—a very wiggly food."

"Okay, I'll eat them first," I say to Isabelle. "As long as you do it too."

Isabelle crosses one eye in.

I do my best chicken impression. "Bawk, bawk, bawk!"

"Go jump in the deep fryer." She shoves past me so she can sit next to Jewel. My sister copies everything my uncle's girlfriend does. Almost everything. Our mom won't let Isabelle get a lightning-bolt tattoo on her arm.

I sit next to Uncle Ant.

"Dimples is out of control," my mother says,

★ SCAB'S BUG COUNTER ★

THERE ARE 1,462 DIFFERENT KINDS OF EDIBLE bugs on Earth. Here's what I've eaten so far:

★ four chocolate-covered crickets—crunchy!

★ two dead flies on a dare from Doyle

★ one mosquito; it flew into my mouth at camp

★ the front half of an earthworm
  (at least, I hope it was the front half!!)

sighing. "One of these days that dog is going to hurt a child."

"A bad dog is the sign of a bad owner," I point out in my most responsible voice.

"He's been reading Doyle's dog books again," groans my sister.

Uncle Ant winks at me. He knows how badly I want a dog. He turns toward my mom, who is tossing the salad. "Remember that dog we had as kids, Molly? We'd throw an old shoe and he'd play fetch until it was too dark outside to see—"

"You mean Roscoe?"

He snaps his fingers. "That's the one!"

"First of all, that mangy dog wasn't ours. He belonged to the Horkheimers down the street. But we did take care of him while they were on vacation. That dog chewed up everything in the house, including my ballerina doll, my plaid scarf, and my favorite straw hat. He ate my lucky shamrock plant, too. Then he threw it up on my bed."

Uncle Ant grimaces. "Oh, well—"

"And that wasn't an old shoe you played fetch with, Ant. That was my best pair of black party sandals. I'd almost forgotten about that horrible animal . . ."

Ker-splat! The salad bowl lands in front of me. A radish tumbles out.

"Sorry, kid," whispers my uncle.

My mom says Uncle Ant has been around too many pest-control chemicals for too many years. She says he's lucky to remember his own name. I don't tell her that sometimes he forgets that, too. If she knew, she would never let him pick me up from soccer practice.

I stab the radish with my fork.

"So how is our girl genius?" Jewel asks Isabelle.

"She got an A on her science report," says my dad. He is in the den, peeking under the sofa cushions.

"An A-plus," corrects Isabelle. "I did it on microfossils. You know, ancient bacteria, seeds, and pollens."

"Interesting," Jewel says in that way people talk when they are really not that interested.

"Stromatolites are three-point-five billion years old," Isabelle says. "They are formed by cyanobacteria, which use sunlight to convert carbon dioxide and water into energy. They release oxygen into the air to support life on our planet—"

"Your breath kills life on our planet," I cut in.

"Shut your trap, Scab."

"Trap your shut, Isabelle."

"Kids," warns my mother.

"I am writing a report on bats," I tell Jewel.

"Did you know bats pee hanging upside down?"

She laughs and shakes her head.

"We're going to the night house at the zoo for *my* birthday party," I say.

It is tradition for Isabelle and me to have three birthday parties. First we celebrate our birthday together with all of our cousins, aunts, uncles, and grandparents. Then Isabelle and I each get a separate party with our own friends. We tried having a party with all of our friends together once. It didn't work. Girls go radioactive if you fling even a little fudge frosting on their Hello Kitty shirts.

"You want to come with us and see the bats whiz?" I ask Jewel.

"Sure, why not? What are you doing for your party, Isabelle?"

"I . . . I don't know."

My head jerks up all by itself. She doesn't know? What does she mean, she doesn't *know*? Isabelle always knows what she's going to do for her party. Shoot, she plans every detail a whole year in advance,

★ INCREDIBLE BAT FACTS ★

I READ THERE ARE MORE THAN NINE HUNDRED different kinds of bats in the world. The Malayan flying fox is the largest bat on Earth. It has a six-foot wingspan! Bats are good for the environment. They eat tons of insects. At night a bat can eat six hundred to one thousand bugs every hour! I don't think my uncle can eat nearly that many.

right down to the color of the jelly beans. I watch my sister pick apart her napkin. Isabelle only tears paper when something is bothering her.

"You had a great time at Laura's lemon tea party last year, remember?" My mom brings a plate of chicken wings to the table. "It was so darling, Jewel. It was a lemon theme—lemonade, lemon pie, lemon cookies. They even played Pin the Lemon on the Tree."

"Did they rip some lemon belches?" I ask.

My mom shoots me a "keep quiet, young man" glare. "Naturally, all the girls wore yellow party dresses. That was fun, wasn't it, Isabelle?"

"I guess."

"We could make cucumber sandwich cutouts with the cookie cutters. You could invite Laura and Kendall, and some of your new fifth-grade friends—"

"No."

"But why—?"

"Because I don't want to," snaps Isabelle. "Tea parties are kind of last year, Mom."

"All right. Well, you think about it." My mother looks around the kitchen. She peers into the den. "Where is your father? Jason, are you coming? It's time to eat."

My dad walks into the room. He's holding his eyeglasses. "That's strange."

"What is it?"

"I can't seem to find a single bottle of my lens cleaner anywhere."

CHAPTER

6

Have a Nice Day ☺

I hear something," says my sister. "Do you hear something?"

Bug spit! If those supersensitive ears of hers figure out that the noise is coming from my backpack, she is going to ruin everything.

"It's the engine," I say. "These school buses are older than our parents. We could explode in a ball of fire any minute—"

"No." Isabelle scoots to the edge of the green seat. "It's not the engine."

We hit a bump. My backpack flies upward. I throw my body over it.

Ms. Rigormortis stops the bus. That's not her real

name. But she looks like a skeleton with a sheet of skin stretched over her bones. Doyle's mom runs a funeral home so I know that rigor mortis is when a dead body goes stiff. Ms. Rigormortis always stares straight ahead with her skeleton hands clamped to the steering wheel. I am certain she is one of the undead.

Kids are getting on the bus. There's Reece Perez and Isabelle's friend Laura Ling . . .

★ IS YOUR BUS DRIVER A ZOMBIE? ★

DOES YOUR BUS DRIVER YAWN A LOT? ZOMBIES NEVER get enough sleep.

Does your bus driver wear pants that are too short? Zombies have no fashion sense.

Does your bus driver have a big Thermos of coffee? Zombies like coffee.

Does your bus driver always seem to have a cold? Zombies have no immune system.

If you answered yes to most of the above questions, your bus driver is probably one of the undead.

"Sloshing," says Isabelle. "That's what it sounds like—water sloshing."

I put my arm over my backpack. "Aren't you going to sit with Laura?"

She lifts her chin. "No."

I glance back. Laura is sitting five rows back with Veronica Oliver. Veronica only talks to a few people—mostly popular girls. Never boys. She once went to a private school and thinks she is too good for public school. She wears polka dots every single day. There's only one reason why Laura is sitting with Snotty Polka-Dot Pants back there.

I nudge Isabelle. "So Laura and you had a fight, huh?"

"No, we didn't."

"Then why didn't Laura say hi when—?"

"Zip it, Pilobolus." Isabelle moves across the aisle to an empty seat.

I have *got* to look up that word to find out more. I have a feeling it's going to be my name for a long time.

The microphone crackles. "Stay seated while the bus is in motion," Ms. Rigormortis says without emotion.

For the rest of the ride to school, Isabelle stares out the window.

"Have a nice day. Have a nice day." Ms. Rigormortis says the same thing to every kid that gets off the bus. "Have a nice day. Have a nice day."

I never say anything to her. Nobody does.

Like always, Doyle is waiting for me when I hop off the bus. We walk quickly, but not too quickly in case Super Spy is tailing us.

"It's all set," says Doyle. "The guys are waiting behind the orchestra portable. I've made them promise to keep everything top secret. I've made sure the area is clear of all teachers and playground monitors. It's secure."

I salute him. Doyle is good with details, which makes us the perfect team. I am the one with the guts to fly off Alec's Super Colossal Dirt Bike Ramp. But Doyle is the one who makes sure the ramp is long enough, strong enough, and wide enough for me to do the stunt. When we get to the portable, four guys are waiting there. I know Andy Quizzenpost and Jake Barton, but I don't know the other two kids. They must be fifth graders. Doyle hands out the bottles of Isabelle's Smell. I collect the money. "Thank you, come again," I say as I take their dollars.

"I've got four more orders," whispers Doyle once the guys leave. "Plus, I'm talking to a couple of sixth graders at first recess."

"Sweet!"

My best friend holds out his hand.

I slap his palm. "I'm out of spray bottles and bolo— I mean, a few things. I'll have to go to the store

★ SCAB'S TIP #26 ★

Best friends make the best team.

★ 59 ★

after school for stuff to make a new batch."

"Gotcha." He's still holding out his hand.

I look at it. "What?"

"Well . . . it's just that . . . you've made twenty-seven dollars, so far."

"Yep." That's almost half a new dog!

"I . . . I was wondering . . . uh . . . when do I get my half?"

"Your half?"

"Of the money from Isabelle's Smell." He sees the look of shock on my face. "What's the matter?"

"Doyle, it's just that . . . you know I'm trying to save as much as I can as fast as I can for my dog."

"Well, sure, but—"

"And I thought that since you have a dog already, you wouldn't mind—"

"I mind, all right. Dogs aren't cheap, you know. I have to buy him treats and toys, and I'm saving up for one of those cool doghouses with a tin roof."

My chest starts to ache. Can't Doyle understand that I want those things too? Doesn't he see that I'm miles and miles behind him? I only want to catch up. Why won't he let me catch up?

"Half seems a lot," I say. "How about a buck a bottle? That's fair."

"A buck? We always split everything down the middle, Scab. I thought we were a team."

"We are, but—"

"But what?"

"Doyle, it's my invention."

"Is not."

"Is so."

"Who dug around in your stinky garbage cans? Whose dog gave you the secret ingredient? Who's been working like crazy to get all these orders?" He pounds his chest. "Me, that's who. You'd be broke now if I hadn't told the guys about Isabelle's Smell. It's only fair that I get an equal share—"

"Wart!" I hiss, spit flying everywhere. I pull Doyle behind a post. We don't say a word until Mrs. Lipwart goes through the big red doors into the school.

Doyle jerks out of my grasp. "Do I get my half now or not?"

"Not!" It's my turn to do the chest pounding. "It's *my* invention."

Doyle balls up his fist and for a minute I think he is going to hit me. His eyes drill into mine. His cheeks are turning

★ **SCAB'S TIP #27** ★

BEST FRIENDS MAKE THE BEST team, unless one of them is a selfish Erdnusskopf.

blister red. I stare right back. I don't blink. I don't flinch.

"Forget it. Forget you." Doyle swings at air. He stomps off toward the building. "Go buy yourself a new best friend."

"Couldn't do any worse than you!" I yell back.

Nobody cheats Scab McNally, especially not greedy, seedy, slimy, grimy former best friends who can't blow a decent snot bubble without my help. If I live to be 105, I'll never talk to Doyle Ferguson again.

"And you can keep your stupid dog poop," I scream. "I'll find my own!"

The red door slams shut.

A kindergartner in a lime green jacket is staring up at me.

"What?" I shout.

He takes off running.

CHAPTER

7

A New Partner?

It's weird being in the lunch line without Doyle. We like to pretend to wrestle until Mr. Hibbolt tells us to "straighten up and act like gentlemen." That's my cue to let out an enormous burp, which always makes Doyle laugh.

★ WILD BURP FACTS ★

Did you know the loudest burp ever recorded sounded like a jet aircraft taking off? Everybody burps about ten times a day. If I chug a whole can of soda pop at once, I can burp "Yankee Doodle" straight through!

★ EVEN WILDER FART FACTS ★

YOU FART ABOUT FIFTEEN TIMES A DAY (AND MAKE two cups of foo-foo gas)! Alec toots twice that much (he isn't allowed to buy chili in the cafeteria anymore). Farts can travel at ten feet per second. Whew! I read that termites are the largest producers of fart gas. Remind me to tell that to Uncle Ant before he eats his next batch of bugs.

Should I buy sausage pizza or spicy chili? The pizza tastes good, but the slices are tiny. If I go with the chili, I'd get a big bowl. Plus, I could let some chunky farts fly at Cloey Zittle during math. *Fla-hooey!*

I go for the chili. I pay for my lunch. I turn around. Doyle is already sitting at our table with Will and Alec. He's claimed my second and third best friends for himself. Bug spit! I can't go over there now. A drop of sweat dribbles down my back. Everything is a blur. Kids are rushing past me to get to their friends. I feel smaller. Not on the outside. Inside, I mean.

"Scab!"

Just hearing my name, I grow a whole foot. On the inside.

"Hey!" Isabelle is waving a hunk of corn bread at me. I am glad to see her. Don't tell her I said that.

Isabelle is sitting at the last table in the last row by the window. Normally, she eats with Laura and Kendall, but they are not around. Again. My sister seems to be spending an awful lot of time by herself. I want to ask what's wrong, but I don't. She'd only call me a *Pilobolus* and tell me to mind my own business.

"You can sit with me until you patch things up with Doyle," says my sister.

"How did you know—?" I stop. Stupid question. She is, after all, Super Spy.

"What's the fight about?"

"One of my inventions."

"Then it's a dumb fight."

"How do you know?"

"I've seen your inventions. You should tell him you're sorry."

"But I'm not." I don't need Doyle or his stupid

dog. Mr. Dawber's sheepdog, Grizwald, lays plenty of dog cookies. I can make Isabelle's Smell all by myself. And I can sell Isabelle's Smell all by myself. However, Doyle was right about one thing; to get a dog there is one person's help I *do* need. . . .

I clear my throat. "Isabelle?"

"Yeah?"

"I'm going to ask Mom and Dad for a dog."

"Again?"

"This time I'll have sixty dollars."

"You do?"

"I *will*. But I need your help."

★ WHY DOGS RULE ★

★ Dogs lick your face. Cats lick their butts.

★ Dogs want to curl up with you on your bed. Cats want to ralph up a furball on your bed.

★ Dogs want to learn tricks. Cats want to sleep.

★ Dogs love you. Cats love you if you've got a can of tuna.

"I'm not loaning you—"

"I don't want money."

"Then what?"

"Could you tell Mom and Dad that you want a dog too?"

She moans. "Scab, I—"

"You know you want a pet as much as I do. Does it really make a difference if it's a cat or a dog?"

My sister picks at her corn bread.

"All you have to do is help me get them to say yes. I'll do everything after that. I'll feed him, play with him, walk him—"

"You?" She snorts. "You? You, Scab McNally, will scoop poop?"

"Yep. I've already scooped Oscar's. I'm pretty good at it too."

She looks impressed.

"So will you do it? Please, Izzy? Please?"

"Hey, hey, what's that smell?" Lewis Pigford is behind my sister. "Hey, hey," he calls out, "it's Isabelle!"

I slump down. One row over, Henry Mapanoo and a few other bologna heads are laughing it up.

"He's been doing that all week," Isabelle says to me.

"Your stuff is primo, Scab," says Lewis. "Primo! It worked great."

I keep sliding. My head is now barely visible above the table.

Isabelle has one eyebrow up.

Lewis lets out a whoop. He puts a hand to his ear. "Hey, hey, what's that smell?"

"Hey, hey," his friends shout back, "it's Isabelle!"

"Smelly Isabelly," sings Lewis. He dances in a circle and kicks out his legs. "Smelly Isabelly."

"I'd better go," says Isabelle. Her face is a splotchy pink. "I was going to practice my violin anyway."

"Wait," I cry, popping back up. "What about—?"

"We'll see," she says, gathering her stuff on her tray. She gets up. "In case you're interested, Doyle hasn't stopped looking at us since you sat down. You should go tell him you're sorry."

"But I'm—"

"I know, I know, you're not sorry. But he's your best friend, Scab. You guys fit together like puzzle pieces. You don't want to lose that." She looks past me. I follow her gaze. Ah! There they are. Laura Ling and Kendall Peters are sitting two rows over. Have they been there all this time?

"Why didn't you—?" I try to ask her why she didn't sit with her friends at lunch, but Isabelle is already making her way down the row.

Lewis is still doing his silly dance. "Bye, Smelly Isabelly. Bye," he bellows after her. "See ya, Smelly. La, la, la . . . Smelly Isabelly . . . dee, dee, dah . . . Smelly Isabelly . . ."

I want to tell that prunehead to leave my sister alone. But Lewis Pigford knows too much. He could

DOYLE AND SCAB:
★ A FRIENDSHIP TIMELINE ★

★ **SUMMER AFTER SECOND GRADE:** Doyle and I meet at Camp Vashon. I show Doyle how to float on the lake. I teach him how to fart in the water too. Team Daredevil is born. Follow the butt bubbles!

★ **THIRD GRADE:** Doyle and I get put in different classes, but we play and eat together every day.

★ **SUMMER AFTER THIRD GRADE:** Doyle goes to spend the summer with his dad in Dallas. It is the worst three months of my life. Doyle's, too.

★ **FOURTH GRADE:** We both get Miss Sweeten. Hooray! The Daredevil Boys are together again.

★ **MIDDLE OF FOURTH GRADE:** Our friendship ends. Bummer.

spoil everything. I am inches from getting a dog. Inches. So Lewis keeps singing and Isabelle keeps walking and I keep silent.

My stomach hurts. And it's not from the chili.

CHAPTER

8

The Killer Fart in Room 242

ave a nice day." Ms. Rigormortis's drab voice follows me off the bus.

"You, too," I say. I don't know why I say it.

I look back. Ms. Rigormortis is smiling. Sort of. She's wearing a green retainer thingy in her mouth. I guess even zombies want good teeth.

I hop off the last step. I feel great. No, I feel *incredible*! In my backpack, I carry three bottles of Isabelle' Smell. Once I sell these, I will have earned sixty dollars! All I need now is for Isabelle to agree to—

"Scab?"

★ SCAB'S LIST OF DOG NAMES ★

- ★ Bruiser
- ★ T-Rex
- ★ Scamp
- ★ Otis
- ★ Mad Max
- ★ Black Ninja

Warning! Super Spy radar has locked on to me again.

Slowly, slowly, slowly I turn. "Uh, huh?"

Isabelle catches up to me. "Okay," she says. "I'll do it."

"You mean—?"

"I'll tell Mom and Dad I want a dog too."

Yes!

My sister points at me. "But you have to feed him."

Yes!

"And you have to walk him."

Yes!

"And I get to name him."

NO!

"Isabelle, you can't—"

"That's the deal. Take it or leave it."

When it comes down to it, I guess having a dog named Princess Bonbon Fancypaws is better than no dog at all. Right? So I say the only thing I can say. "Take it."

★ **ISABELLE'S LIST OF DOG NAMES** ★

★ Miss Kiki

★ Peaches

★ Lady Lollipop

★ Cookies-n-Cream

★ Precious Puddles

★ Kevin

Isabelle grins. "When do we ask?"

"Tonight."

"You know, Mom and Dad *still* might say no."

"They won't." How could they? I'll have the money and my responsible sister on my side. What could go wrong? It's going to happen. I am really going to get a dog! I want to jump a mile up into the air. But I don't. I don't dare slosh now. Once my sister is gone, I do a victory lap around the monkey bars on my way to the orchestra portable. Sweeeeeeet!

I am the first one to show up. I am supposed to meet Elliot Parkhurst, Thor Bryant, and a sixth grader named Rocco with a blue streak in his hair. I kick a plastic cup around in a figure eight while I wait for them to show up.

Brrrrring!

That's the first bell. I decide to stay until the second bell. Of course, that means I will be tardy. I start pacing. Before long, I wear a path into the gravel.

Brrrrring!

Second bell. Still no sign of the guys. Bug spit!

I try to sneak into class when Miss Sweetandsour's back is turned.

"Scab McNally, you're late."

How does she do that?

"Put your backpack away and take your seat, please."

Doyle lets out a cackle when I pass his desk. He tries to kick me. He misses.

"You're such a *Pilobolus*," I say. Gently, I place my pack on the bottom shelf. "You probably don't even know what a *Pilobolus* is, which makes you a dumb *Pilobolus*."

"You're the only fungus around here," he hisses.

I give him a whopping raspberry. I really let it blow through my lips. I sound like a garbage truck.

"Quiet, class!" Miss Sweetandsour glares at me. "It's time for morning announcements."

Each day a different student from the audiovisual club gets to read the school bulletin on camera. It's broadcast to every classroom in the school through closed-circuit television. Doyle is in the AV club.

★ SCAB'S TIP #11 ★

Never take a test . . .

★ first thing in the morning, when you are sleepy.

★ before lunch, when you are hungry.

★ after lunch, when you are sleepy.

★ at the end of the day, when you are hungry.

On second thought, avoid tests altogether.

He's a pretty good reader, too. Miss Sweetandsour turns up the TV. Felice Pryor speaks very softly. She holds the paper in front of her so we can't see her face. We all lean forward to hear. When the news is over, my teacher says, "Clear off your desks and take out a pencil."

Bug spit with extra sprinkles! We are having a social studies quiz.

Cloey taps me on the back. She hands me a note. It's from Elliot.

Where were you?

I write:

Behind the orchestra portable. Where were you?

He writes back:

In the bathroom with Thor and some weird kid with blue hair.

Oops. I forgot to tell them where to meet me. Doyle usually handles that stuff.

I write:

Meet me behind the orchestra portable at first recess.

As I am folding the note, Miss Sweetandsour snatches it away. "You'll be staying in first recess, Scab."

HOW TO EARN BIG
★ TEACHER'S-PET POINTS ★

★ Help your teacher collect homework papers.

★ Raise your hand first to answer a question (even if you don't know the answer). Your teacher will almost always call on the kid who is trying to hide under his desk.

★ Tell your teacher she looks nice even if she's wearing the giraffe-print dress that makes your eyes crazy.

★ Bring your teacher an apple instead of a garter snake.

"I can't. I have to—"

"It's not a request."

I get a C-minus on my quiz. Miss Sweetandsour asks for a helper to hand out the geography workbooks. I rush to the cabinets in the back of the room. I need mega teacher's-pet points today.

"Ouch!" I feel a sharp pain in my side.

It's Doyle's bony elbow. He tries to take the pile of workbooks from me.

I pull the books toward my chest. "I'm doing it. Back off."

"You back off." Doyle pulls back.

"I was here first." I tug again.

"Teacher picked me." He tugs again.

"Doyle Butt Boil."

"Go pick yourself, Scab."

I yank hard.

He yanks harder.

Haven't I done this before with a certain wiener dog?

"Hey, guys," says Will. "Come on, don't fight."

"Nobody's fighting," I snarl. "Just tell him to let go."

"Me?" snaps Doyle. "You let go."

"You first."

"No, you."

"You."

"You!"

"Okay." I give him a smirk. Then I let go.

Doyle teeters on his heels. His arms go up. His rear goes down. Workbooks fly everywhere. Doyle's mouth forms a giant O a second before he crashes into the shelves. The bottom shelf pops loose. Backpacks, purses, lunches, and hats start tumbling out. Some slip down the shelf like they are riding a water slide. Everything lands on top of Doyle.

I laugh so hard my stomach nearly explodes. The whole class is laughing too.

Doyle's got a yellow mitten on his head. A zebra-print raincoat is attacking his chest. A brown blob wobbles on the front of his jeans. It looks like chocolate pudding. I sure hope that's what it is.

"Did you hear that?" says Doyle. He fights off the zebra raincoat.

I am still howling. I wonder if Will caught that on his camera phone.

Doyle rolls over. "Wuh-oh, Scab."

I see my backpack. It's squashed flat. I stop laughing. Doyle and I exchange looks. He tries to get up but slips on a silver purse.

I reach for my backpack. But it's too late.

"Ewwwww!" cries Meggie Kornblum. "What's that smell? Miss Sweeten, something stinks back here."

Cloey Zittle points at me. "It's Scab."

I put up my hands. The backpack hits the floor. "It's not me."

"Scab cut an atomic fart!" announces Lewis.

"That's powerful thunder!" shouts Henry. "My eyes are stinging."

Mine, too. There's a lump in my throat. I start to cough. Kids are leaping out of their seats. Some are running toward me. Most are running away.

Miss Sweetandsour is at the intercom. "This is

room 242. Uh . . . we have a situation here. Some sort of powerful odor. . . . Yes, yes. . . . Clear the building."

"I can't breathe," yells somebody.

"I can't see," calls someone else.

The fire alarm goes off.

"We're going outside," Miss Sweetandsour calls above the shriek of the siren. "Remember how we practiced? Move quickly. Stay calm, students."

Nobody is listening. Nobody is staying calm. Books and pencils fall off desks. Feet tromp down the aisles. Kids are crying and choking and screaming.

"Somebody get my lunch!"

"Somebody get the hamster!"

"Miss Sweeten, Lewis is turning green!"

"Let's go. . . . Everyone out. . . . Single file," yells our teacher, waving. "Quickly. Quickly."

I can't move. My feet won't go!

Something latches on to my wrist. Through burning eyes I see Doyle's face. He hasn't forgotten me. I should have known he wouldn't. We're the Daredevil Boys. No matter what, we are a team. Isabelle is right. We fit together like puzzle pieces.

"Follow me, Scab!" shouts Doyle.

"Where's Will?"

"He's already out. Let's go."

"We're going to die," Cloey screeches in my ear. "Scab's fart is going to kill us all!"

CHAPTER

9

This Just In . . .

★ BREAKING SCAB NEWS ★

BY ISABELLE C. MCNALLY
(RIVER ROCK SPELLING BEE CHAMPION)

★ 8:37 a.m.: Scab snuck behind the orchestra portable before school again. It was the third time this week he'd done it. I knew he was up to something.

★ 9:59 a.m.: The school fire alarm went off. A mysterious stink was coming from room 242—Scab's classroom.

★ 10:04 a.m.: I caught up with Scab out on the soccer field. He told me he didn't know a thing about the smell, but he wouldn't look at me. Something was definitely up.

★ 10:28 a.m.: Firefighters dressed in white suits and helmets went into our school. The news reporters called them hazmat, which stands for "hazardous materials team." One of the hazmat guys brought out a black backpack with a silver lightning bolt on the flap—Scab's!

★ 10:46 a.m.: I overheard a policeman talking to reporter Naomi Marcus of Channel 7 Action News (I love her). He told her the stink came from a bottle of homemade perfume by some kid named Scar.

★ 10:47 a.m.: Lewis Pigford told Naomi the kid was actually Scab. He said it wasn't perfume at all. It's a sister-repellant spray named after ME! He said Scab was selling the stuff to kids at school. Lewis Pigford is a TAPEWORM! So is my brother.

★ 10:48 a.m.: Lewis threw up on Naomi's boots. ☺

★ 10:55 a.m.: Scab disappeared. Good thing. When I find him, he's roadkill!

★ 11:01 a.m.: Mr. Huckabee closed school for the day so the hazmat team could air out the school. He was looking for Scab too. Mr. Huckabee was so mad, his head looked like a shiny, red balloon.

THIS CONCLUDES SCAB NEWS FOR TODAY. Isabelle Catherine McNally reporting.

P.S. 12:14 p.m.: Naomi Marcus is on the noon news talking about Isabelle's Smell.

P.P.S. My life is over.

CHAPTER
10

Zombie with a Heart

I climb onto the bus. I fall into the first seat behind the driver. On the way to school Ms. Rigormortis keeps looking at me in her rearview mirror. I wish her black zombie eyes would stare at somebody else. I pick at a rip in the cushion.

"Where is your sister?" she finally asks in her blah voice. "She hasn't been on the bus all week."

"She's fine," I say.

My sister won't go to school because she's afraid everybody will tease her about Isabelle's Smell. I've tried to tell her I am sorry. She won't let me in her room. She screams through her bedroom door, "Go away, Pilobolus."

Ms. Rigormortis is looking at me again. "Tough year," she says.

I sigh. "No kidding."

"I meant for Isabelle."

Isabelle, Isabelle, Isabelle. Everyone is worried about Isabelle. Uncle Ant and Jewel came over and brought my sister a gold heart necklace. My mom made ziti, Isabelle's favorite food. What about me? I'm the one who has to clean desks every single recess for two weeks. I'm the one who has to write a five-hundred word essay about being a responsible

student (I don't even know five hundred words). I'm the one who had to give back every dime I earned selling Isabelle's Smell. Worst of all, I'm the one who won't be getting a dog EVER! So it's only fair that I should be the one at home now. I should be wolfing down strawberry ripple ice cream. I should be crying into my butterfly pillow—I mean, you know, if I was a girl. You *know* what I mean.

The bus turns into the school parking lot.

"Have a nice day," Ms. Rigormortis says without emotion as we leave. "Have a nice day. Have a nice day. . . ."

I don't say anything back.

After school I go to my sister's fifth-grade classroom to pick up her homework. Mr. Corbett hands me a folder and Isabelle's notebook. "I hope she'll be back soon. Your sister is doing great in my class. Just great. I know it must have been a challenge to get moved up a grade this year."

"Not for Isabelle," I say. Nothing is a challenge for my sister.

"In my fourteen years of teaching she's one of the brightest students I've ever had. You must be very proud."

"I guess," I say. I hadn't thought much about it before. I mean, Isabelle doesn't need me to be proud of her. She's got our parents, Uncle Ant, her teachers, and pretty much the entire population of Granite Falls. What difference does it make what I think?

When I get outside, it's raining. The first bus is pulling away from the curb. Oh, no! Mine is fourth in line, but the door is still open.

"Wait for me! Wait, number eighteen! Ms. Rigor—" My toe finds a crack in the sidewalk. *Splat!* I go down. Isabelle's homework folder lands upside down on the wet pavement. The wind scatters the pages. I scramble to my feet. I run, trying to scoop up papers as I go. My sister's notebook is floating in a puddle. I grab it. The bus door hasn't closed yet. I can make it. I *can* make it! Holding everything tightly to my chest, I run faster. I can see the edge of the sidewalk. Leap. *Leap now!* I launch myself off the curb. I am flying, flying, flying—

★ OOEY GOOEY ★

IN TEN HOURS OF CLEANING DESKS AND TABLES,
I found:

★ 27 gum wads

★ 21 spit wads

★ 13 pens and pencils

★ 9 erasers

★ 4 Gummi bears

★ 2 broken rulers

★ 3 half-chewed Milk Duds!

Ker-chunk! My nose hits glass.

I slide down the bus door. I hear a crunching sound. I gag on engine fumes. I am a pile of bones on the ground when I hear it.

Eeeeee-yoe.

The door opens. Ms. Rigormortis is staring straight ahead. She doesn't say anything. Her skeleton hands hold the wheel tightly. I stagger up the steps. I don't want to sit behind her, but it's the only seat left. My nose throbs. I think I broke my face.

I lay out all the loose papers on the seat. I try to put them back in the right order. The folder is bent and dirty. I hope I got everything. I'm shaking the water out of my sister's notebook when I see a big red X. The ink is runny, but I can still read what is written beneath the X:

> *I hate the fifth grade. The fifth grade hates me.*
> *I hate the fifth grade. The fifth grade*
> *hates me. I hate the fifth*
> *grade. Everyone*
> *hates me.*

The red words are bleeding into one another. I slam my sister's notebook shut. I wish I hadn't read it. No, that's not it. I wish the words she'd written weren't true. But they are. Something inside me knows they are.

What if I was wrong? What if getting moved up a

grade *has* been a challenge for Isabelle? Not for her brain, I mean, but for her mind. And for her heart. Everything is starting to make sense now: my sister playing alone, my sister eating alone, my sister riding the bus alone. Isabelle is stuck. She's trapped between the fourth grade she left behind and the fifth grade that won't let her in. Doyle and I are puzzle pieces. We fit perfectly. But Isabelle doesn't fit anymore with anyone. And what do I do? I come along with my stupid sister repellant and make everything worse.

I clutch Isabelle's notebook to my chest. Black zombie eyes are watching me in the rearview mirror. "Tough year," says Ms. Rigormortis.

This time, I nod.

CHAPTER

11

A Bold Idea

No, Mom. I'm not going—"

"Isabelle, you have to go back to school sometime."

"Why? So Lewis and his friends can call me Smelly Isabelly? No, thanks."

I poke my head into my sister's room. "Pretend Lewis is me, and zing him the way you're always zinging me—"

I get beaned in the head with a butterfly pillow.

"Like that."

"Don't talk to me, Pilobolus," yells Isabelle. "Tell him not to talk to me, Mom."

"Isabelle Catherine, you have exactly fifteen

minutes to get dressed and be downstairs," says our mom. "I'm driving the two of you to school. Scab, is your essay ready?"

"Yep."

She turns to my sister. "Fifteen minutes."

In the car Isabelle draws a droopy flower in the steam on her window. She chews her lips the way she does when she is trying to keep from crying.

"Isabelle, I—"

"Don't talk to me."

"I know what *Pilo*—"

"You don't know anything." My sister covers her ears with her hands. Her window flower fades away.

At school I go to the office. I have to give Mr. Huckabee my essay on responsibility. Mrs. Lipwart tells me to sit in the chair outside his office. I start kicking the leg of the chair. I snap my fingers while kicking the leg. I whistle while snapping my fingers while—

"Scab McNally!"

I stop.

"How long you in for?" Doyle is beside me.

I wave my paper. "Just dropping off." I look him over. "You?"

"It's my turn to read the morning bulletin."

"Oh."

Doyle shoves his hands in his pockets.

I go back to lightly kicking the leg of the chair.

He digs his toe into the corner of a broken tile.

This is crazy. "Doyle," I burst out. "I'm sorry I didn't give you your fair share of money. I'm sorry I said all that stuff. I'm sorry—"

"Me, too." He cuts me off.

We both take a deep breath and grin. I put out my hand. He puts out his. We do our secret handshake. End of fight. Neither one of us likes fighting. Our longest argument lasted seven days, three hours, and ten minutes. I forget what it was about. I only remember it lasted forever.

"Too bad about your spray," says Doyle. "Maybe your next invention will—"

"My parents shut down my lab."

"For good?"

"Nah, but long enough. Two weeks."

Doyle winces. "Sorry."

"The worst part is . . ." I swallow hard. I can't say
it out loud. I can't.

Mrs. Lipwart is waving a piece of paper. "Mr. Ferguson, the bell is about to ring."

My best friend starts to shuffle away. He spins. "Scab, you want to walk Oscar with me after school?"

"Okay." I smile.

It's good to have someone who knows you from the bones out.

Doyle takes the bulletin from Mrs. Lipwart. He goes into the tiny TV studio next to the copy room. It has a small window. I can see him adjusting the video camera. Everything at River Rock stops for the morning news announcements. Maybe I should join the AV club. Imagine having everybody's attention all at once. Wouldn't it be cool to have every single teacher and every single student listening to every single word you say—

I bolt up. I've got an idea.

Doyle is clipping on his microphone. The first bell rings.

My hands are sweaty. My heart speeds up.

If I'm going to do this, I have to do it now. When Mrs. Lipwart answers the phone, I slide my essay under Mr. Huckabee's door. I sure hope he understands. If not, I'll be scraping Milk Duds off the bottoms of desks until I go to middle school.

She's worth it.

★ DAREDEVIL BOYS' ★
SECRET HANDSHAKE

★ **STEP ONE**: Clasp thumbs.

★ **STEP TWO**: Wiggle fingers.

★ **STEP THREE**: Slap palms.

★ **STEP FOUR**: Knock knuckles.

★ **STEP FIVE**: Bang your chest with your fist.

★ **STEP SIX**: Burp 'em if you got 'em.

CHAPTER

12

Off Wiener Sand

"See that red light on the camera?" asks Doyle. "When it goes on, you're on."

"Got it." I sound like a frog. I'm thirsty. And I really gotta pee. I hop up and down. I *am* a frog.

The red light blinks. I stare at it.

"Scab? You're on!"

"Oh . . . hi, everybody out there at River Rock. Um . . . I'm . . . uh . . . Snab McScally—I mean, Scab McSnally. Oh, bug spit! You all know me. I'm Scab. Uh . . . I'd like to say I'm sorry for stinking up the school last week. I'm even sorrier—is that a word? My sister would know. She's the person I'm sorrier to,

if that's a word. Izzy, you were right. I am a *Pilobolus*. That's a fungus that grows on cow poop, everyone. I read all about it in a science book I checked out of the library. See, it shoots out these tiny spores and they fly like little rockets right over the cows. They blast off at something like thirty-five miles per hour and can scatter something like eight feet. Wicked, huh?"

Doyle is making a circle in the air with his finger. I don't know what that means, so I just keep going. "Anyway, I'm really sorry to everyone, especially Isabelle, for being such a *Pilobolus*. And I guess that's pretty much all I wanted to say, so . . . uh, I guess I'll just say *off wiener sand*. That means 'good-bye' in German, right, Isabelle? Oh, and Miss Sweeten, it looks like I'm going to be tardy again. . . . Are we still on the air?"

A lunch tray lands across from me. A sesame-seed bun slips off the top of a sloppy joe sandwich.

"It's pronounced 'owf vee-der-zay-in,' you fruit bat, not 'off wiener sand.'"

Not exactly what I was going for, but at least my sister is talking to me.

Isabelle slides into the seat next to Doyle. "I can't believe you let him go on TV like that."

Doyle shrugs as if to say, "It seemed like a good idea."

Isabelle takes a cautious look around the cafeteria. "Kids are *never* going to stop teasing me now."

Sitting next to me, Will jumps in. "He was only trying—"

"I know, I know." Isabelle's eyes look red and tired.

I don't know what to say. I have made things worse again. Bug spit!

"Isabelle?"

I turn my neck. Jenna Lucas and Libby Miles are standing behind me. Posing, is more like it. The fifth graders in Isabelle's class want to be models. How do I know this? Because they are always putting on fashion shows at recess. They pretend the courtyard is a runway. They line up and strut around the square like supermodels. You may hurl chunks now.

"Are you okay?" Jenna is asking my sister.

"Uh . . . yeah." Isabelle is covering her mouth as she tries to swallow a bite of sloppy joe.

"You poor, poor thing," sighs Jenna. She gives me a frosty look. "It's bad enough that you made that nasty spray, but then to go on TV and embarrass your sister all over again. . . ."

"I didn't mean—"

"The nightmare that is Scab continues." Libby pops her gum.

"Brothers are such a pain," says Jenna. "I have two of them, so I know what you're going through."

"We should sell our brothers to the zoo or the circus or something," adds Libby. I chuckle at her joke. But she isn't laughing.

"Tell me about it," my sister mutters under her breath. "It's all right," she says to the girls. "I'll be all right."

"You are an absolute rainbow," says Jenna. "Isn't she a rainbow, Libby?"

★ CRACKING THE GIRL CODE ★

WHAT A GIRL SAYS	WHAT A GIRL REALLY MEANS
I don't have a pen you can borrow.	I DO NOT want your slimy, disgusting boy germs on my cute, fuzzy, turquoise troll pen.
Did Miss Sweeten say you could do that?	I'm tattling on you right now!
I got chosen to be a library helper.	You are a big, hairy butt wart.
I got an A++ on my social studies test.	You are still a big, hairy butt wart.
Stop bugging me and read the directions.	Stop bugging me and read the directions.

Libby nods, folding another stick of gum into her mouth. Boy, can that girl chew cud. "Scab, you're lucky to have such a nice sister."

"I know," I say seriously. I smile at Isabelle.

My sister's lips turn up at the corners. Just a sliver. But it's enough.

"If it had been me," Libby spits, "I would have turned you into onion rings at exactly eight fifty-five this morning." Still, no laughter. I slowly scoot myself and my lunch tray the other way.

Libby whispers something to Jenna, who whispers something back. They go back and forth a few times, before Jenna says, "Let's just ask Isabelle and see—"

"Ask me what?" my sister chimes in.

Is that spit on the side of her mouth? Is my sister drooling?

Libby stops chomping. "I know this is probably not your thing, but . . . I mean, we were thinking that if you weren't busy helping Mr. Corbett tutor the slow kids at recess that maybe you'd like to . . ."

Isabelle leans forward. "Yes?"

Yep, that's slobber, all right.

"Do you want to be in our fashion show?" blurts out Jenna. "You're probably not even into clothes—"

"Are you kidding?" she squeals. "I love clothes."

"You do? Really?"

Clearly, Jenna is surprised that Isabelle would have room in that superpowered brain of hers for something so totally stupid. Never fear. She does.

Isabelle's head has turned to rubber. It's bouncing all over the place. "Really. I love modeling, too. I watch all the modeling reality shows on TV."

Jenna strikes a new pose. "Fa-bu. You're in the show. Meet us at the courtyard when the bell rings."

"I can't make it," I say, waggling my fingers. "I'm having my nails done. Then I'm going to be a rainbow. Will and Doyle, do you want to be rainbows too?"

Doyle burps.

"I'd rather be a butterfly," says Will.

Our laughter is interrupted by the whack of Libby's backpack strap against my neck. The sting sends goose bumps up my arms.

"We're going to go remind Perri and Kayla," says Jenna. "So we'll see you in about twenty minutes?"

Isabelle's mouth breaks into a full grin. "Fa-bu."

★ **SCAB'S TIP #14** ★

Never mess with a girl who can shove her whole fist in her mouth. Or yours.

Suddenly Libby is very close to my left ear. I smell watermelon. She cracks her gum. It echoes through my skull. I shiver. "Tomorrow," she hisses, "she's eating with us. Got it?"

"Got it." I rub the rising welt on the back of my neck. I'm not scared of much in this world, except swimming where I can't touch the bottom, automatic sliding doors, and food that's folded. You may now add one more thing to that list: Libby Miles, Boy Hater.

The girls walk away practicing their runway strut. It's enough to make a guy lose his lunch. But Isabelle is happy. I know because she doesn't lose that goofy grin even after I cram two carrot sticks up my nose and try to blow them out.

"Wuh-oh," says Doyle.

Isabelle and I follow his gaze. Lewis Pigford is dancing this way.

"Wuh-oh," I say.

"Let's go," says Doyle. Isabelle, Will, and I start throwing stuff on our trays. But it's too late.

Lewis is already singing. "Hey, hey, what's that smell?"

Isabelle is shrinking behind her sloppy joe and salad.

"Hey, hey, it's Isabelle!" Lewis has got his arms up in the air and is swinging his hips like a belly dancer.

"Cut it out, Lewis," I say. "Izzy, don't pay any attention to him."

"I'm fine," croaks Isabelle. But her hair is in her eyes and the smile is gone. Isabelle tosses her napkin on her tray. "I'd better get ready for the fashion show—"

"Smelly Isabelly. Smelly Isabelly . . ."

My sister untangles herself from the bench. She stands up.

I try again. "Don't go, Izzy—"

"Smelly Isabelly. Smelly Isabelly."

Isabelle grabs her tray.

"Izzy, you shouldn't let him—"

"Smelly Isa—"

"Smell this, Lewis." My sister swings around. She pushes her tray straight into Lewis Pigford's chest. Lewis freezes. Kids gasp. The tray falls to the floor with a ear-splitting clatter. The room goes deathly still. Lewis's light blue T-shirt is now a sliding collage of gooey hamburger meat, barbecue sauce, and bits of lettuce and tomato. Is that ranch dressing or blue cheese on his neck? Hard to tell. Lewis's jaw drops. His arms hang in the air. His hip is still jutted out to one side, mid–hula dance. He can't believe it. None of us can. This is Isabelle. Straight-A+, teacher's pet, spelling bee champ, first-chair violin Isabelle. I have never been prouder.

★ SCAB NEWS ★

BY ISABELLE C. MCNALLY
(FIRST-CHAIR VIOLIN)

★ 7:37 a.m.: Scab put salt in my orange juice. Again!

★ 8:29 a.m.: Scab picked the dirt out of his belly button all the way to school and made a giant lint ball. GROSS!

★ 8:52 a.m.: Scab told me he was sorry for naming his stinky spray Isabelle's Smell, which was pretty cool. Unfortunately, he said it on TV in front of the entire school, which wasn't so cool. Talk about embarrassing!! I was about to drop out of school for good, but then Jenna and Libby talked to me. They actually spoke to me at 12:06 p.m. today! I have been waiting all year for this miracle. They said they understood what it was like to have an irritating brother. Jenna has two of them!! I guess it took a lot of guts for Scab to apologize to me on TV. Did I just write that? Did I just write that Scab did something without thinking of himself first? Another miracle! That's two in one day.

★ 12:22 p.m.: Scab called me Izzy again. I told him not to do it anymore. I don't think he will forget. ☺

THIS CONCLUDES SCAB NEWS FOR TODAY.
Isabelle Catherine McNally reporting.

P.S.: Mom and Dad, I need to talk to you about something
REALLY important!

My sister picks up her backpack. Calm as anything she says, "And for the millionth time, Scab, my name is Isabelle."

Everybody watches my sister stroll out of the cafeteria.

Lewis watches a sesame-seed bun slip-slide down his shirt.

Hello, Isabelle. Off wiener sand, Lewis.

CHAPTER
13

Scab's Lab, Part 2

F reedom!" Doyle yells into the phone.

"Freedom," I yell back. As of today, my lab is no longer off-limits. I'm an inventor once again. Sweet!

"So what are you working on?"

I look at my drawings. "I'm inventing a minicannon that shoots gumdrops. You catch them in your mouth. I call it Pilobolus Candy-obolus."

"Cool!"

"You want to help me build it?"

"Sure, unless you have to go."

"Go?"

"Uh . . . didn't you . . . uh . . . say you were going somewhere?"

"No."

"Oh, then yeah, okay, I'll come over."

"Scaaaaaaaab!" That would be my sister. Isabelle must have found the dead grasshoppers I put in her jewelry box. They've been there for two hours. It's part of my experiment to see how long it takes your sister to find dead insects in her jewelry box. She's getting much better at finding my experiments.

"Isabelle's coming," I tell Doyle. "When you get here, I'll be in the cave—"

"Wait!"

"What?"

"Maybe you're . . . uh . . . not in trouble."

"What do you mean?"

"Yeah, maybe Isabelle wants you for . . . you know, another reason."

What he is talking about?

"What are you talking about?"

"N-nothing."

Oh, it's something, all right. I can tell by his voice it's something.

"Doyle, what's going on?"

"I don't know."

Yes, he does.

"And even if I did know, I couldn't tell you."

Doyle is trying to keep a secret. Lucky for me, my best friend can't keep a secret.

"Does this have something to do with my birthday?" I press.

"I . . . uh . . . I gotta go."

It does!

"Scaaaaaaab!" Isabelle's in the hall. I've got exactly three seconds to pry this secret out of my buddy.

"Come on, Doyle. You've got to tell me—"

"I . . . I . . . can't. Just promise me one thing."

"What?"

"You'll never live it down with the guys. No matter what happens, no matter what she says or how she begs, you've got to promise—"

"What?"

"Spit-swear you won't—"

"What?"

"No pink collar! Okay? Do you promise? Uh . . .
Scab, are you there? *Scab?*"

Just when Scab thought it was safe

to go back in the water . . .

FOLLOW SCAB INTO

THE DEEP END IN

SeCReTS
of a LaB Rat

MOM, THERE'S A DINOSAUR
IN BEESON'S LAKE,

COMING NEXT SPRING

FROM ALADDIN!